Praise for Cindy Procter-King

"Cindy Procter-King is a master storyteller. Not only do her characters invite the readers into the drama, the humor is non-stop. Comedy is a hard genre to write but Cindy Procter-King does it easily."

— The Road to Romance on HEAD OVER HEELS

"What a set-up for a comedy of errors! Everything that can go wrong in this scenario does go wrong, and the reader is well entertained by the comedic chaos."

— Fallen Angel Reviews on HEAD OVER HEELS

"*Getting Over Brett* is a top-of-the-line read. It has everything you could possibly want in a modern romance. It's fun and playful at times, full of flirty banter, then deeply romantic and emotional at its heart. Somehow, it's both sweet and sexy all at the same time!"

—Julianne MacLean, USA Today Bestselling Author

"Cindy Procter-King presents readers with a suspenseful snapshot of a romantic comedy... loaded with humor, this is a must-read."

— Night Owl Reviews on PICTURE IMPERFECT

"Procter-King has written a 'home' for all of us. Destiny Falls is the place that holds your first love, your first triumph..."

— RT Book Reviews on WHERE SHE BELONGS

Deceiving Derek

Also by Cindy Procter-King

Steamy RomCom

Love & Other Calamities

RomCom Series

Catching Claire (Book 2)

Before Brady (Book 3)

Just Janie (Book 4)

Trusting Trey (Book 5)

Love in the Pacific Northwest

Stand-alone Romantic Comedy

Head Over Heels (Book 1)

Borrowing Alex (Book 2)

Getting Over Brett (Book 3)

Contemporary Romance

Deceiving Derek

CINDY PROCTER-KING

Blue Orchard Books

DECEIVING DEREK

Published by Blue Orchard Books

Cover by The Killion Group

ISBN: 978-0-9880884-4-3 (eBook)

ISBN: 978-1-989113-05-9 (Print)

For my parents, who've celebrated more than 65 years of marriage through life's ups and downs

Chapter One

Friday night, July 14th

Countdown to Tania and Trey's wedding: 15 days

(unless...)

"Someone is stealing my underwear! You need to find out who."

Detective Derek McAllister arched an eyebrow and lifted his gaze from his computer screen in Rosevale's police station. A woman in her twenties stood on the other side of his desk. Waves of fluffy blond hair framed her delicate features, and a slinky red dress hugged her slim curves. Chin at a haughty tilt, she dangled a scarlet G-string six inches from his nose. Her hand wobbled. The scrap of racy underwear flipped off her fingertip, slid down the side of his Mariners coffee mug, and puddled onto his notebook.

"Hello," Derek responded in a polite voice. "How did you get back here?" He glanced around the woman toward the front counter several feet away. Biggs—the balding desk sergeant—plus Harding, a lanky patrol officer who shadowed Biggs like a starved-for-attention sidekick, looked back at Derek and chortled.

Biggs twirled a finger near one cauliflower ear. "Friday night goof," the stocky man mouthed.

Derek resisted the urge to roll his eyes. *Passing the buck, huh?* It figured with that duo.

The two uniforms were covering the night shift. While Derek had reported a slow afternoon, plenty of work remained before the bars closed and mid-July activity hit the streets. Consider Harding. Instead of scrolling through his personal socials on his phone, the dope could check parks and alleys. As for Biggs, reading department emails should take precedence over playing Sudoku and chatting up the curly-haired clerk, who was doing her best to ignore him.

The visitor at Derek's desk stared him down.

"Well?" Her blue eyes shooting sparks, she planted a hand on her hip. "Are you going to shuffle me off like they did"—her fingers flicked toward Biggs and Harding—"or take me seriously?" Her hair shimmered to the shade of golden honey beneath the precinct lights.

Derek drew in a breath. Taking initial theft reports wasn't his responsibility. His job was to investigate. But frazzled nerves radiated off the woman. Given the odd nature of her complaint, he wanted to get a good sense of the problem and who she was, so he wouldn't need to conduct a second interview later. If her personal safety appeared at issue, he'd rather address her concerns and escort her home than direct her back to the men up front. Sending her away to roam the Rosevale streets in her agitated state was out of the question.

Elbows on his desk, he hunched forward in his swivel chair. Expression neutral, he eyed the G-string. He slipped a pen beneath a flimsy strap and lifted the panties as carefully as if he were handling a piece of forensic evidence. "Is this the underwear in question, ma'am?"

"*Ma'am?*" she echoed. "Do I look eighty?" She glanced away and cleared her throat. "You may call me Ms. DeMarco," she said, looking at him again.

"And no, Detective McAllister. That isn't the underwear I'm talking about. That underwear isn't missing. *Is* it?"

Derek swallowed a smile. Something about Ms. DeMarco's righteous ire piqued his interest. At another time—but especially in another place, like at a bar or a party—he might inquire whether she wore any underwear.

But tonight was not the time. And the Rosevale Police Department on the outskirts of Seattle definitely was not the place.

"All right," he replied. "Ms. DeMarco. Might I ask what underwear of yours *is* missing?" Unless his hearing had forsaken him, she had specified *her* underwear.

She snatched the panties off his pen. "My lingerie designs. The prototype samples." She shook the G-string. "This thong is a prototype too, but thankfully the thief didn't nab it."

Derek's lips quirked. "Are you sure there was a thief?"

"Yes, Detective McAllister," Ms. DeMarco said with strained patience. "You are Detective Derek McAllister, right? That's the name she—I mean, the men at the counter gave me."

Derek arrowed another glance to the front. Biggs

looked over his shoulder and snickered. Harding scratched his stomach beside his uniform buttons.

Derek returned his gaze to his complainant. He tapped his pen on the nameplate near his computer. "The officers are correct."

Ms. DeMarco's jittery gaze tracked his movements. Shoulders squaring, she looked him dead in the eyes. "Okay, Detective McAllister. When a burglary occurs, a thief is involved. Can we agree on that?"

"Yep." Unless this poor woman had imagined the episode. Anxiety hopped off her body like ants attacking a sugar bowl. Should he contact another authority?

"Then let's get cracking." She hoisted an oversized shopping bag off the floor and plunked the sack onto his desk. She dug inside and withdrew a lingerie top. Ms. DeMarco tossed the G-string and top beside his computer before rummaging through the bag a second time. "Damn it," she grumbled.

Her nose scrunched in an appealing and endearing manner. Although why Derek allowed himself to think of this woman in anything other than a professional capacity while she sought his help at the Rosevale PD tested his powers of reasoning.

He needed to end the inappropriate thoughts ASAP.

Several pink undergarments and a floaty nightie flew out of the bag. "I wanted to make sure he—I'm pretty sure the thief is male—didn't steal more samples, so I grabbed as many as possible before catching the bus over here. The problem is these pieces take up so much room I'm having trouble finding my wallet." The sack coughed up a purple bra and a pair of silky mint-green panties.

Derek put down his pen. "Don't worry about the wallet." Did she think she had to pay him?

She lifted a finger. "Wait! I see it." She emptied the bag until an explosion of frothy colors littered his desk, reminding him of his twin sister Janie's rooftop garden after her ex-boyfriend broke her heart and she'd weed-whacked every petal.

It occurred to him Janie would like Ms. DeMarco. He visualized the two of them annihilating blossoms side by side.

"Aha!" Ms. DeMarco produced a slim wallet. A phone clattered out of her bag, clunking his penholder. Amid the chaos, she peeled open the wallet, extracted a business card, and shoved the card into his hands.

Derek scanned the stylish script on cream-colored stock: LACEY'S LITTLE UNDERTHINGS. LACEY DeMARCO, CEO.

"Lacey?" he muttered, tossing the card onto his keyboard. "Give me a break." Was he being pranked?

A blush splashed her face. "That's right. Lacey DeMarco. My mother, Christiana DeMarco, is the famous lingerie designer out of Milan. My sister is Silken, and my brother is Teddy. Our mother believes in theme names."

"Does she?" Derek pressed down another smile. He'd never heard of Christiana DeMarco, which wasn't a stretch. Fashion wasn't his thing. "Look, Ms. DeMarco. I need to understand the situation." He sifted his fingers through the lingerie heaps. "If someone is stealing your underwear, what's this?"

She gazed at the mounds. "This is what's left. What I've rescued."

"Uh-huh. From the thief?"

"Yes." Her voice rose. "No one has stolen this lingerie." She tossed the phone back into her bag. "Yet."

"Gotcha." Derek selected a pair of panties and studied the inside stitching. The fine needlework read, LACEY'S LITTLE UNDERTHINGS. Just like her business card. Maybe his complainant was on the up-and-up. "Okay." He tossed her the panties, which she caught with surprising deftness. "Please sit." He indicated a chair to her left. On his computer, he saved a draft of a grid of vehicle thefts. "Tell me what happened." He opened a new report.

She remained standing. "I'd rather tell you on the way over."

"On the way over where?"

"My place."

"*Your* place?" He shook his head. What now?

"My design studio is in my apartment. That's where the theft occurred. Don't you want to inspect the crime scene?"

"I'll take notes first."

Her eyebrows jumped. "We don't have time! What if he strikes again? He's already plundered me twice."

"The panty thief?" Derek asked against his better judgement.

"The corporate panty *raider*," Ms. DeMarco responded. "Lacey's Little Underthings is a legitimate company, Detective McAllister. You've seen my business card. I have a website. I demand your respect." She danced a fingertip along the top of his computer. "Lacey's. Little. Underthings," she enunciated as if she were scolding a misbehaving preschooler. "Look it up."

Derek thumped a spiral pad against his palm. The vehicle-theft grid could wait. Ms. DeMarco deserved his attention and protection as much as any other Rosevale citizen. Even if he wasn't technically on duty.

"Give me a minute." He pushed back his chair and walked to the counter. "Harding, I need a ride-along. Are you available?"

The guy slipped on his police hat. "Negative. Just got a call."

Biggs stepped away, palms out. "And I need to write a report."

Derek nodded and glanced over his shoulder. At his desk, Ms. DeMarco shoved handfuls of lingerie into her bag.

Derek scratched his cheek. All right. He would poke around her design studio, call in the crime scene techs if necessary. Volunteer an hour toward securing her peace of mind, tops.

He crooked a finger, beckoning her forward. "Not to worry, Ms. DeMarco. I'll be happy to take a look."

Chapter Two

Lacey risked a sideways glance at the handsome plainclothes detective sitting behind the wheel of the unassuming mid-sized car. Exhilaration raced through her veins as he maneuvered the vehicle through Rosevale's twilit streets.

She'd done it! She had really done it! Earlier tonight, when Alicia had read out the most challenging item on the scavenger hunt list—one police officer—every guest at Tania's bachelorette party had groaned. Except for Lacey.

Thanks to her new friend Janie McAllister's devious skullduggery, Lacey would drag this sexy cop to the festivities and win the scavenger hunt. *Yee-haw!* Staid-and-boring Lacey DeMarco had lived her last days. A work-hard-but-play-harder Lacey had been born.

A sliver of guilt wriggled beneath her skin. She shifted on her seat, adjusting the hem of her daring new dress and angling another glance at this gorgeous specimen of male pulchritude. Derek shared his twin sister Janie's ash-blond hair and stormy-ocean gray eyes.

Lacey wrinkled her nose. *Ugh.* Why couldn't he sport a wart on his forehead? Or treat her like gum in his hair? Or exhibit other troll-like behavior? Anything to combat his attractiveness.

She gazed out the tinted passenger window, scanning the buildings and holding her breath until her cheeks filled with air. *Okay*, she conceded to her tenacious inner conscience. Maybe it was a trifle uncool that Derek's sister Janie had peeked at the scavenger hunt list while Lacey and Alicia had decorated for the party. Neither was it fair to the other guests when Janie had whispered where and when Lacey might locate her brother, who, Janie had said, wouldn't cooperate if he suspected Lacey's visit to the precinct was a lark.

But Janie had volunteered to assist Lacey on her quest to liven up her life. What was livelier than convincing a hottie cop to attend the event?

Being an overachiever had its limits. For Lacey, learning to break free of her shell meant coloring outside the lines now and then. She'd made great strides this summer. Tonight was her ultimate test.

"Take a right at the next corner," she instructed the detective.

"I'll use my GPS." He eyed the dashboard screen. "What's the address?"

She fluttered her fingers. "It's not far. Just follow my directions."

He slid her a suspicious glance. "Is there something you're trying to hide?"

"No." She squeezed her hands together on her lap. She didn't want him realizing the location of her studio at this stage of their adventures, that was all. She huffed. "Can't we do this my way?"

His gaze lingered on her wringing hands. "Fine." The car slowed as they approached a red light. "When did you notice your designs were missing?" he asked in a deep voice that rolled over Lacey like a warm wave.

She ran her palms over the skirt of her dress and smiled. Her dream to market her lingerie designs to nationwide acclaim had come in handy. She'd fabricated the story about her mother and invented the siblings but her plans for Lacey's Little Underthings were real. Her rejuvenated image would boost her confidence for next week's meeting with a group of Seattle investors.

"About ten days ago," she answered in all honesty. Her friend Alicia, tonight's party host, lived across the hall in their apartment building. Lately, whenever Alicia popped in for girl talk, her old dachshund in tow, several of Lacey's lingerie samples had gone missing. It had taken her forever to solve the mystery.

At first, she'd thought someone *was* stealing her samples. Then she'd discovered them buried in the pile of discarded fabrics Alicia's dog burrowed in to nap during visits. As a result, Spats was no longer permitted access to the small second bedroom Lacey used as her studio.

The traffic light turned green. "Any idea who the thief might be?" Derek asked as the car motored down the street.

Derek. Lacey sampled the sound of his name in her mind. Not out loud. God forbid. He might consider that weird. With his muscular build, the intelligence Janie had remarked upon, and the intensity Lacey had noticed when he'd glanced up from his computer, they would make beautiful babies together.

Babies? Her pulse bounced around at the base of her throat like a steel ball in an old-fashioned pinball machine. Sure, she wanted a family and a career. But if she ever planned to become pregnant, unless she decided to visit a sperm bank she needed to start dating again first.

A furrow formed on Derek's forehead. "Ms. DeMarco? My question?"

"Oh. Yes. You can call me Lacey." As her fantasy baby-daddy, he possessed every right.

"Okay. Lacey, I asked if you have any ideas?"

Did she ever! But each suddenly revolved around slipping into her latest black satin Merry Widow design and dragging Derek the dashing detective to bed.

"Um, yes. I have a suspect." She pointed out the turn to her mid-century apartment complex. "My mother's design rival, Spats—" Forcing a cough, she broke off. It wouldn't do to give her mother's fake nemesis the same name as Alicia's pet. Spats lived with Alicia. The dog was *at* the party. "Sorry, mentioning the guy freaks me out a little." She fished around in her brain for a believable story. Alicia had inherited Spats from a great-aunt. The elderly woman had named Spats after the cad who'd trampled the lady's romantic dreams into dust. What was the asshat of a heartbreaker's name?

"Pietro?" Lacey whispered, glancing out the window. "Spatafora?" Her eyes widened. That was it! "Spatafora," she repeated, looking at Derek again. "Pietro. Yes."

One of his eyebrows lifted. *Amazing*. He could really do that. Few people could.

"Have you confronted Mr. Spatafora?" he asked.

Of course she had. The canine version. Hence the closed door to her studio.

"No." She braced herself against the additional lies. "Pietro is short but fierce." The dog was short, at any rate. She had no clue about the human. "And he carries a grudge." Lacey gave her head a firm shake, as if she couldn't believe the tale herself. "After all these years, Pietro hasn't forgiven my mother for marrying into the DeMarco family dynasty instead of running away with him." A whopper of a falsehood born of desperation.

"I see," Derek responded in a tone conveying that he didn't see at all. He steered the car into the parking lot for her three-building complex.

"Yes. They were involved long before I was born. My mother gave him up for my father's money, and Mr. Spatafora has been intent on revenge ever since." Lacey jabbed a finger toward the nearest empty spot. "That's my space." Another untruth. She couldn't afford a car, much less rare on-surface parking. "Pull in here."

Derek parked the vehicle. Before he changed his mind about his investigation, Lacey flung open her door and climbed out. She adjusted the straps of the shopping bag on her shoulder.

The soles of Derek's shoes scraped asphalt. His perceptive gaze catalogued the area. "How long have you lived here?"

"Four months." Now that was the absolute truth.

Derek rubbed a thumb beneath his lower lip. "I might have visited this complex before. Building C."

Lacey picked a thumbnail. Alicia had previously lived in building C. Inheriting Spats had required a move to building B, the only one of the three that accepted pets.

She waved a hand. "You know how it is. These old developments look identical. It's easy to confuse them." She pursed her lips. "Did you bring your badge?" She should have checked for his Rosevale PD identification at the station. What if other party-goers requested proof of his profession?

Nodding, Derek patted the waistband of his jeans.

Lacey's gaze lowered, and her mouth dried. Derek's police badge sat kind of close to his zipper. His very interesting zipper, which bumped out nicely where—

Her tummy warmed, and she looked up at his face. Where she *should* be looking.

"Excellent," she said, her heart galloping at what felt like ten million beats per second. Derek's twin sister could vouch for him. His gun holster and the handcuffs hooked on his belt offered further confirmation that Lacey had produced a real, live police officer.

He smiled. And what a smile it was. Luminescent and pearly. Too bad he wouldn't stick around once he realized Lacey had deceived him.

He looked at the pavement. "You dropped something." He retrieved the siren-red thong.

Lacey's cheeks burned. "Thank you." She reached for the panties. Her hand brushed his, and his gaze settled on her face. Heat swamped her lower body. *Oh, my.*

Inhaling a shaky breath, she faced her building.

Too, too bad he wouldn't be sticking around.

Chapter Three

DEREK COULDN'T STOP SNEAKING peeks at Lacey's curvy behind as he trailed her along the fourth-floor hallway. Her tale about Pietro Spatafora? Pumped full of holes big enough to swallow his unmarked police cruiser. But the wiggle in her red dress distracted him like a rookie juggling a donut and a steaming cup of joe. His shift had ended hours ago. He supposed it wasn't too far out of line that he'd grabbed a break from inputting his report to investigate her story.

"We're almost there," she said, casting a smile over her shoulder that kindled a glow inside his chest. His sister Janie often hassled him about getting a life outside of police work. Not two hours ago, as he'd chowed down a burger at his desk, Janie had texted him flak about spending another Friday night at the station. Maybe his twin was on to something. He hadn't dated in months. No earth-shattering reason. The women he'd met hadn't intrigued him. Other than the one walking in front of him.

Lengthening his stride, he caught up to Lacey. She sent him another heart-stopping glance.

Yep, under different circumstances, Lacey DeMarco was the sort of woman he pictured getting a life *with*—provided she walked on the right side of the law. They could have some humdinger times, he and this lively blonde with her infectious smile and sparkling eyes. Lacey was an original. Derek had sensed that from the moment they'd met. What other woman had ever strewn underwear on his desk? He had the distinct impression life with Lacey DeMarco would never be dull.

A ruckus boomed from an apartment. Stopping at the door, Lacey gnawed her lip.

Derek cocked an ear. "You left on music?" The noise sounded like stripper songs. Did the sexy tunes inspire her designs?

"Ummm." She passed the shopping bag from hand to hand.

"It's a little loud," he advised. "Don't your neighbors object?"

Her nervous laughter tinkled in the empty hallway. "Not this neighbor."

He narrowed his gaze. "What do you mean?"

"Derek." She spoke his name softly and slowly, as if she were licking an ice cream cone. Or something else. "What's behind this door might come as a surprise."

He smiled. So far, everything about her had come as a surprise. "What kind?"

"You'll see." Sucking in a breath, she opened the unlocked door. Not big on security, he noted. A red flag.

He followed her into a small living room. Raunchy music pounded in his ears, and colorful streamers swooped down from the ceiling as balloons bounced on the striped sofa and off the walls. A dozen women danced and clapped to the melody. In the middle of the cheering throng, a half-naked dancer in an approximation of a police uniform gyrated his hips to the erotic wail of a saxophone belting from a music dock.

The stripper ripped off his costume pants, revealing a bulging leather G-string—and a phony police badge where no badge should ever reside. The women whooped and hollered like a pack of starving hyenas.

Lacey's eyes bugged.

Derek gestured at the crowd. "This is your studio?"

"No," she shouted above the pandemonium. "This isn't my apartment. I live across the hall."

"What?" He shook his head. "Ms. DeMarco, we need to talk." Somewhere quiet where he could dig to the bottom of whatever was going on. He gave the party another look. "Either in your apartment or down in the lobby. Not in here."

"We can't leave!"

"Why not?"

"Because of..." The music drowned out her words. "...and Pietro Spatafora."

"Pietro is here?" The stripper couldn't be the alleged thief. Lacey had said Pietro was short, and the dancer looked big *everywhere*. Derek's retinas fried each time the dude busted a move.

Lacey didn't respond. Thrusting her shopping bag into his hands, she bee-lined for a petite redhead wearing a toilet-paper getup over jeans and a wedding-themed T-shirt. Derek hustled after her.

She grabbed the redhead's arm. The woman stumbled away from the stripper.

"Lacey!" The woman's eyes widened. "Woo-hoo, you're back!"

Lacey flapped a hand toward the dancer. "Tania, who brought that guy?" she shouted above the music.

"Claire rented him for me," the woman named Tania yelled back. A balloon bobbed against her shoulder. "Isn't he to die for?" Tania giggled. "Forget marrying Trey. Ridge can frisk me whenever he wants." She snorted.

Lacey frowned. "Is this your way of saying Claire won the scavenger hunt?"

Tania's eyes crossed. "Huh?"

The dancer gyrated toward Derek and the two women, bumping balloons out of his path.

"The scavenger hunt," Lacey repeated close to Tania's ear. "Did Claire win?"

A small burp popped out of Tania's mouth. "I dunno. Ask—" Tania grinned as the stripper patted her arm. She nodded, and he dragged her back into the throng of screaming women.

Derek gritted his teeth. A stripper named Ridge and a scavenger hunt? What kind of party was this? "Lacey, what's going on?"

She squinted at the other women. "Ridge doesn't count. He's not a real cop." She glanced at Derek. "You are."

His lips pulled down. "What am I, a party favor?"

"Um, more like an item on a scavenger hunt list."

"Unbelievable." He squashed the shopping bag beneath his arm. A bra jutted out, and the wire thing under the cups poked his armpit. "Then your story about the panty thief was to get me here under false pretenses?"

"What?" Lacey curved a hand around an ear. "I can't hear you with all this noise."

Derek leaned forward. His lips grazed her soft hair. "Pietro Spatafora," he murmured. "Is he real?"

She nodded. "In a way."

She steered him around the cheering partygoers and opened a bedroom door. A snoring wiener dog —Ridge's scaled-down sidekick?—napped half under a pink hoodie in the middle of a double bed. Lacey left the door open a crack. A yellow balloon trickled into the room, and the stripper music slowed to a crawl.

Lacey stepped toward the dog, flourishing a hand. "Detective McAllister, this is the dachshund previously referred to as Pietro Spatafora. Pietro is real, but I don't know where he lives, and it's not important. He was a means to an end. The dog's name is Spats." Her shoulders lifted in a shrug Derek wished didn't look so damn cute. "Spats belongs to my friend, Alicia. You might know her. This is her apartment."

Derek's head spun. Should he know this Alicia ? "Then the panty thief—?"

"Was Spats."

"And your mother isn't Christiana DeMarco?"

"No. Her name is Catherine. She's a pharmacist in Briarton." Lacey named a neighboring Seattle suburb. "Silken and Teddy are fake names. For pretend siblings. I'm an only child."

He heaved out a sigh. "Is *your* name Lacey?"

A sweet smile blossomed on her lips. "Yes."

Derek tossed the big shopping bag onto the bed. The dog exhaled, his front legs stretching. Derek crossed his arms. "Ms. DeMarco, I'm a police detective. We deal with criminals. Bad people. Do you understand? We don't have time to waste on a wiener dog with an underwear fetish."

She winced. "It's like this—"

"Calm down, little brother," a familiar voice interrupted from behind him.

Derek's neck stiffened. *Janie.*

He should have known.

Lacey's heart sank like a boulder plunging into an ice-cold lake. Derek the dashing wouldn't want anything to do with her after this! At least Janie had returned. She would help Lacey explain.

Derek whirled to his sister. "Janie? What the hell?"

"Wait a second," Lacey said, touching the detective's corded forearm. Her fingertips tingled. "Janie?" she asked her friend. "Derek is your younger brother?" she attempted to clarify. "I thought you two were fraternal twins." In other words, the same age.

Janie pshawed. "He's younger than me by four minutes. That gives me big sister interference privileges." She smiled. "Lacey, this is me getting you a life." Janie pantomimed a curtsey. "You're welcome." Hands on hips, she gazed at Derek. "Getting *both* of you a life."

Noise erupted in the living room. Through the open bedroom door, Lacey glimpsed other scavenger hunt enthusiasts returning with their booty. Some carried cop dolls in raised fists.

"I have a life," she protested to Janie.

Derek scowled. "Ditto."

"Right," Janie responded with a fair dose of sarcasm. "All either of you do is work. Derek, Rosevale is enjoying its lowest crime rate in years, but you run around like gangs are infiltrating the area."

"That's what they pay me for...big sis."

Lacey shook her head. "I'm confused." She looked at Janie. "I realize I spend too much time alone in my studio," she implored her friend, "but I'm trying to step out of my comfort zone. Thanks to your influence, I'm way more assertive. Example, the scavenger hunt list said, *police officer*. I brought Derek. As a member of the Rosevale PD, he qualifies. Claire cheated with the stripper stunt. I win."

Janie snickered. "*I* cheated. I convinced Alicia to add 'police officer' to the list. We agreed to show you the items ahead of everyone else."

"Oh," Derek mumbled. "That Alicia."

Lacey shot him a glance. "You know her?"

"We've met once or twice."

"Three times," Janie amended. "I thought it was a fabulous match, but Alicia said dating my brother gave her hives." Janie grinned at Lacey. "You and my twin might stand a chance. The stripper surprise was a coincidence. The cop bit was a setup to get you and Derek together."

Lacey's mouth dropped open. Yeah, Derek was hot. And handsome. And honorable. But Janie had leapfrogged over an important point. "You wanted to set us up after Alicia said dating him gave her hives?"

"Hey," Derek said. "I'm in the room."

Janie ignored her twin. "Alicia's dad and brothers all work in law enforcement," she explained. "She's had it with overprotective alpha guys telling her what to do."

Derek's hand sliced the air. "That's not how it happened with Alicia and me. She's nice. We just didn't hit it off in the way you wanted, Janie. End of story."

Janie grinned again. "End of one story. The beginning of another, better story about a creative lingerie designer and a cranky but tolerable cop." She placed her hand over her heart. "My brother, who I love despite his lack of twin ESP." She whispered behind a hand to Lacey, "He's not always crabby."

"Only when I'm being played," Derek groused.

Lacey swallowed past a lump in her throat. Her romantic chances with Derek didn't appear too hopeful, which filled her with alarming sadness. She hadn't been looking for a relationship, but she liked him. A whole bunch. Despite his irritation with his sister. Regardless that he was an overprotective alpha guy who had given Alicia hives.

A touch of alpha appealed to Lacey. Like in the bedroom. Or if she fell behind on a deadline. She visualized Derek kneeling beside her sewing machine, promising to kiss her *all over* if she was a good girl and whipped up five cami sets before midnight.

Four months ago, she'd moved from Seattle to Rosevale to reap the benefits of a second bedroom and cheaper rent. She'd promised her mom and the design-school friends she rarely saw that she would carve out time for a personal life. Achieve some sort of balance. Honestly, that wasn't asking too much. But then she hadn't lifted her head out of her work long enough to realize that almost half the summer had passed. She was twenty-six. Socially speaking, she needed to get it together.

She leaned toward Derek. "I don't have a problem dating cops," she whispered. "Or detectives." Especially not this one. A warm and buttery feeling enveloped her. Developing a relationship with a guy as intense and focused as Derek might take not only her career but her entire life to the next level.

He smiled at her pronouncement, and her heart folded over in her chest. Yeah, he was next-level amazing.

"Does the cop agree?" she asked him in a quiet voice.

Janie jumped up and down. "The cop better!"

Derek's gaze remained glued to Lacey. "This seems like the perfect time for my sister to leave. Then we can talk."

"I'm going," Janie said, opening the door wider. She muttered a curse as Tania popped in, blocking her way.

Tania's toilet-paper wedding gown floated around her slim hips. "Did someone say cop? Hey, ladies," Tania called into the living room. "Lacey brought us another cop!"

An avalanche of party guests spilled inside the bedroom, as did several bouncing balloons.

Tania chortled. "Will the nice police officer take off his clothes? Ridge is leaving. We want more."

Derek shook his head and whispered something uncomplimentary about his sister.

Janie spread her hands. "Where is Alicia when I need her?"

Tania hiccupped. "In the kitchen with Claire, making me another Mudslide."

Janie slid an arm around Tania's shoulders. "No more Mudslides for you, my girl." Janie herded the sloshed women out of the bedroom. "I've done my part," she said with a nod to Lacey and Derek. "You two can take it from here."

Chapter Four

THE BEDROOM DOOR banged shut behind Derek's sister. Good thing, because he'd been on the verge of throttling his twin. Then *he* would be walking on the wrong side of the law.

After punting a balloon out of the way, he stepped toward Lacey. "I apologize for Janie, seeing as she's incapable of admitting she's wrong. She had no right to set you up like that. She deceived you."

Tiny lines creased Lacey's forehead. "Janie deceived both of us. Worse, Derek, I deceived you. I'm the one who should apologize." Lacey inhaled. "I'm sorry for barging into the police station and upending your night." She sat on the bed and petted the sleeping dog.

Derek rubbed his cheek. "Sometimes a little

upending can't hurt. In fact, I have a hunch it's exactly what I need."

Lacey glanced up, a flicker of hope lighting her eyes. "You don't have to say that to make me feel better."

His heart pinched. "That's not why I'm saying it." Unlike other women his sister had tried to pair him up with, Lacey ignited a fire deep inside him. Wouldn't it be incredible if they built something real together? "Janie and I are close," he elaborated. "I might get annoyed with her, but I love her to death."

Lacey's head tipped. "How often do you see her?"

"Not enough, because of my job. And that's on me." Derek adored his sister, but he usually hung with other police officers while Janie ran with a tight group of girlfriends. Lacey must be a recent addition to her crew. "To be clear," he asked with a smile, "you're not the slightly offbeat woman I thought you were when you dumped lingerie on my desk?"

Lacey's breasts rose and fell in her low-cut dress. "I wouldn't say I'm offbeat. People say I'm different, whatever that means." Her pert nose wrinkled. "I guess it's all the time I spend alone with my designs..."

Derek smiled. Hands in his jeans pockets, he

nudged her sandal with a foot. "Offbeat and different aren't bad. Lacey, what you are is refreshing."

Her shoulders sagged. "It's an act. Your sister was right. I'm a boring workaholic. What if I remain one for life?"

"Boring? Not a chance." Derek stepped closer. "You run a company. You can't slack off and expect Lacey's Little Underthings to succeed." He paused. If he stood any chance with this woman, he needed honesty between them from this point forward. "Please tell me Lacey's Little Underthings is an actual business."

She combed a strand of honey-blond hair away from her face. "Yes. I've had an online shop for a year, and it's been great. But next week I'm pitching my designs to a Seattle investment firm." Her gaze met his. "Derek, this is the chance I've been working toward. I can't blow it. If Clemmons Consulting backs my designs, I'll be the face of Lacey's Little Underthings on a national scale, which scares and excites me. Janie is helping me step outside my comfort zone. Tonight was supposed to be part of that." She plucked the hem of her clingy red dress. "I guess your sister and I took things too far."

"I'll say. But I don't regret that *you* did."

Lacey's mouth curved. "You don't?"

"Nope." Derek sat beside her on the bed. The mattress squeaked, and her shopping bag toppled over. The satiny thong dribbled out, bumping his hip. "I might not approve of Janie's tactics, but she hit it on the nose when she said all I do lately is work."

"Same here. I haven't dated in months." Lacey's cheeks turned pink. "It's embarrassing."

Derek's lips tugged upward in another smile. "Maybe it's time we both learned to let off some steam. Just because my sister played matchmaker doesn't mean we can't go out for dinner or something." His heart raced at the thought.

Lacey's gaze brightened. "I feel the same." She smoothed a hand over her dress. "It doesn't bother you if I'm not as exciting as I might appear?"

"Trust me, I find you plenty exciting." Derek picked up the thong and dangled the skimpy underwear between them. "If I found you any more exciting, I'd have a heart attack looking at you. Which is a corny cliché, but true."

Her eyelashes fluttered. "Then imagine what might happen if you kissed me," she whispered.

Derek let out a low groan. He would love to kiss this beautiful and surprising woman, although he shouldn't allow his lips anywhere near a complainant.

Luckily, he spied a loophole. "As the fates would have it, I am off duty. And this misstep tonight was a prank." He hesitated. "Right?"

Lacey's gaze swept to his. "There isn't a case, Derek."

"No burglary to speak of."

"Nothing but a girl aching for a kiss."

Damn. He couldn't resist her sweetness.

He dropped the thong onto the mattress. Cupping her face with one hand, he kissed her long enough to feel her lips moving in response. He deepened the kiss with an exploratory sweep of his tongue. Desire pulled at him. He wanted a solid chance with this woman.

Her breathing shallow, she broke the kiss. "Wow," she whispered as their foreheads touched.

"Agreed," he murmured. He clasped her hand. "I hate to break this up, but I need to get back to the station and finish my report."

"And tonight is for Tania. I can't run out on her. As much as I want to," Lacey added.

He brushed a thumb along her plump lower lip. "I want to see you soon."

"Tomorrow night?"

"That's too long from now. When does this party end?"

"At the rate Tania is knocking back those Mudslides, I'd say midnight."

"Perfect." The cop in him needed to ask, "Listen, does Tania have a safe ride home?"

Lacey nodded. "Alicia is driving her, and that woman is stone-cold sober. So am I."

Derek grinned. "You're not under the influence?"

"I'm under *your* influence."

He chuckled. Lacey had a great sense of humor, and after some of the gritty cases he'd worked on, he needed more sunshine in his life.

He kissed her cheek. "I'll be at my desk until you're done. Text me."

"Sounds wonderful." She dug her phone out of the bag, and they exchanged contacts.

A knock rapped on the door. Alicia's voice carried through the wood. "Lacey? Sorry to interrupt, but Tania wants to play Honeymoon Horror. You're the only person who knows the rules."

Lacey smiled at Derek, shimmying her shoulders. "That's because I created the game." She called toward the door, "Coming." She looked at him again. "Promise you're not interested in Alicia?"

"I see her as Janie's friend, and that's it."

"But would you be willing to hang out with her occasionally, along with the rest of our group? You know, if you and I work out? Janie and I had a blast today, and Alicia and I are growing close."

He smiled. "That's an easy yes."

"Great." Lacey rubbed his thigh. Warmth spread beneath the denim, heating his skin.

Derek pulled her in for a quick kiss, threading his fingers through her soft hair.

"I need to run to my place for the game props," she said as they stood. "I'll see you later." They shared a deeper kiss. "Should I bodyguard you to the door? The wilder guests might try to convince you to take off your clothes."

He laughed, shaking his head. "I'll barricade myself in here to say goodnight to my sister. I want to thank her for tonight before I describe the horrible outcome in store for her if she ever interferes in my life again."

Lacey smiled. "But tonight was good?"

"Tonight was fantastic."

Lacey's hands tightened on his. "Good luck with Janie. I'll send her in."

Derek dropped a last kiss onto her pretty lips. "I'll say goodbye to you again before I go."

"I can't wait." Her dress swinging at her hips,

Lacey hurried out of the room. The chatter from other party guests drifted through the door, open a sliver. On the bedcover, Alicia's dog yawned and blinked from the hoodie-blanket.

Derek sat on the mattress again and scratched the animal's scruff. "Hey, Spats. How's life?"

Spats sniffed the shopping bag. The dachshund's front paw inched toward the red thong.

"That's not for you." Derek rescued the G-string. The slippery fabric slid between his fingers. He raised an eyebrow. Dare he develop his own underwear obsession and filch the racy panties as a sexy souvenir of the night he'd met Lacey?

He would need to confess to her eventually. Before she hauled him in for questioning. Or wrongly accused Spats.

He glanced at the doorway. No one was looking.

"Okay, buddy," he whispered, scratching the dog's floppy ears. Mischief glinted in Spats's expressive brown eyes. "We're in this together." Two panty thieves on a mission to get him a love life.

He slipped the thong into a front jeans pocket. "Shh." He put a finger to his lips. "Don't tell."

Epilogue

Six days later
Thursday evening, July 20th
Countdown to Tania and Trey's wedding: 9 days
(unless...)

LACEY SQUEALED as Derek wrapped his arms around her hips, hoisted her up, and spun them in her tiny kitchen. Palms on his shoulders, she gazed down at the happiness radiating from his face.

"Baby, I'm so proud of you," he exclaimed, circling them faster.

"I know! I know!" Her view of the cupboards blurred. "*I'm* proud of me."

"Lacey DeMarco, CEO of Lacey's Little Under-things, now financed by the best venture capitalists in Seattle, is my girlfriend!" His deep voice reverberated against her tummy, and desire stirred low in her body. His bold statement of both facts dizzied her. Their promise to be exclusive, agreed to in the middle of last Friday night during long hours of talking, cuddling, and making out at her place in the wake of Tania's bachelorette party, dizzied her. And the spinning dizzied her.

"Derek." She patted his shoulder. "I might barf."

He stopped spinning. "We don't want that." He set her down on her stiletto sandals. "Hey." Grasping her upper arms while she regained her balance, he peered into her eyes. "Are you okay?"

"Yeah." She swiped a wisp of hair off her forehead.

"I'm sorry if I got too enthusiastic." He kissed the spot where she'd brushed away the lock.

"Never be sorry about showing how you feel. I love that about you." Lacey beamed at her sexy cop and boyfriend of less than a week. She felt safe with Derek, as if she'd known and trusted him for years. "My meeting with Claire's bosses was stressful but exciting," she said, filling him in on her afternoon as she tidied her peony-pink pantsuit. "Claire gave me a pep talk before I went in. She was right about the investors. They're smart and approachable. The experience wound up way less shark-feeding-frenzy than I expected."

"That's great." Derek's hands cupped her face, and he covered her mouth with drugging kisses. "Let's celebrate."

He opened her refrigerator and located the bottle of champagne they'd bought the other day for good luck. Lacey admired his butt encased in faded denim as he set the bottle on the counter and reached into a cupboard for two champagne flutes. After another moment of appreciating his shoulder muscles moving beneath his T-shirt, she stepped close behind him.

"Tomorrow, my liaison and I will begin to assemble my team," she said. *Her* liaison. *Her* team. She treasured the sound of those words. She had been on her own too long. In her professional life, but also on the romantic front. "But tonight..." She dipped her fingers into the inside front pocket of her blazer and dragged out a piece of lingerie. She glanced at the thong that had been missing from the bag of samples she'd dumped on Derek's desk last weekend. "You're in trouble," she announced in a firm voice.

"Trouble?" he echoed, glancing around with the champagne flutes in one hand and a corkscrew in the other. He bumped the cupboard shut and arranged the paraphernalia beside the champagne bottle.

"Big trouble." Lacey twirled the thong until it whirred on her finger like miniature helicopter blades. "Because guess where I found this?"

Derek's gray-blue eyes widened. "In your pile of discarded fabrics? Congratulations, Lacey. You nailed the financing for your company *and* cracked the case of the missing panties." He had the audacity to smile. "You've been pretty determined about tracking down one tiny pair of underwear."

She narrowed her gaze. "Oh, you can do better than that." Clutching the thong, she poked his chest. "Yes, I found these never-worn, one-of-a-kind prototype panties buried in my discard pile." After checking in with Alicia and ruling out Spats as the guilty party, because of Derek's pilfering she'd needed to sew another sample for today's meeting. "Strange, these panties weren't in the pile yester-day." She gave his chest another jab. "Or the day *before* yesterday. Or—"

"Lacey," he interrupted, grasping her finger. He slid a pinky along the base of her thumb, eliciting a trail of goosebumps on her arm. "Take pity on me." His hand lowered to twist the thong between their fingers. "I'm a weak man."

Her pulse leaped. "You're a thief," she accused, if whispering the words counted.

"The thief of your love?"

Her insides softened to goo. "Absolutely," she whispered.

Derek extricated the thong from her fingers and tossed the lingerie over his shoulder. The panties landed on the bread box on top of her fridge. Lacey smiled as he slipped his hands around her waist, beneath her blazer.

He placed a tender kiss on her lips. "I vow never to take another of your lingerie samples into evidence again."

"You mean you vow not to tamper with the evidence?" She tried to sound stern, but his large hands molded her rear, distracting her.

"That's right. No tampering with your panties." He whispered into her ear, "Unless I'm served a warrant."

Lacey chuckled. "I'm contacting a judge and bringing you in on trumped-up charges." She hoped she had some of this law-enforcement jargon right.

"No need. We can avoid the courts if you..." He towed open the neckline of her silky blouse. "...show me what's in here." He peeked inside her top. "Pink bra?" His right eyebrow arched.

"Peony pink," she whispered, breathless with need and want. "To match my pantsuit...and my undies."

"Bikini style, hipster, high-cut, or tanga?" Derek asked, showing off his memorization skills. Now Lacey knew why he'd fixated on her new underwear designs while helping her prepare for today's meeting. Apparently, *he'd* developed a fetish.

She cast up a coy smile. "Wanna pat me down and find out?"

"The champagne will get warm," he mumbled against her lips, pushing her blazer off her shoulders. The garment puddled onto the floor.

"I don't care." Lacey glided her hands beneath his T-shirt and tested the warmth of his skin, skipping her fingertips up and down his washboard abs.

"Lacey." He groaned. "I wanted to wine and dine you first."

"We went out for dinner yesterday." Last Friday, they'd craved precious hours together, not a hurried coupling. Until now, their busy schedules hadn't helped. But Lacey could no longer battle the anticipation building inside her. Considering the bulge in Derek's jeans as she fitted her fingers over his arousal, he was having a hard time of it as well. "The bra and panties I'm wearing tonight are handsewn originals," she whispered, traipsing a finger down her blouse and dipping the digit inside her bra. "No other man will ever feast their eyes on this set."

"You know how to seal a deal." Derek scooped her into his arms and carried her into the bedroom.

As he lowered her to the bed, her head cradled on a pillow. She threaded her fingers through the hair at his nape, kissing him.

Their gazes locked. Passion reflected in the depths of his eyes as he removed her sandals one at a time, his movements slow and tortuous.

"So beautiful. So sweet," he whispered, his loving gaze roaming over her body.

Lacey wiggled her toes and rolled her pelvis, inching down her zipper. She reached out a hand and interlaced their fingers. "Don't stop now," she whispered. "Derek, please."

A sexy smile hooked one corner of his mouth. He sat beside her hip. As he leaned over her sensation-swarmed curves, his hands created a protective cage on either side of her head. His fingertips grazed her hair and neck.

"I can't believe how lucky I am," he said. "To have found you." He rained amorous kisses on her mouth.

Lacey squirmed beneath his gentle caresses. "I feel the same way."

"Look at us," he whispered. "Two workaholics... getting ourselves a love life."

Lacey's throat tightened. "Is that where we're headed? Toward love?" She ran her hands along his strong biceps.

"I'm halfway there." His voice emerged on a rough note.

Tears pricked her eyes. "Oh, Derek. Me too." She grappled with his T-shirt. The next minutes passed in a haze of undressing, kissing, and fondling, until their limbs tangled on the bed.

His hands caressed her breasts and tummy. His skillful touch aroused sparks between her legs.

He opened a packet and sheathed his erection. His gaze traveled over her hips and breasts. Sensation danced on her skin as her heart swelled and her center throbbed.

"All for me?" he asked, positioning his body over

hers. His arms supported his weight. His fingers stroked her cheeks, her jaw, her brow.

She swallowed back deep emotion. "Only for you," she whispered. "Derek, every inch of me is yours."

"Every inch of me is yours," he echoed, entering her with a carnal groan.

Lacey gasped with the realization that at this moment, her vulnerability was on full display. No matter how their relationship had started, not one ounce of falsehood could survive the love blossoming in her soul for this amazing man.

His hands brushed her hips and breasts. His fingers inched between her thighs as they kissed and moved.

"I love us together," he whispered in her ear. "Lacey, how much I care about you is hitting me hard."

"I'm falling in love," she admitted, heart pounding. There was no turning back now.

He picked up the pace. "Ah, baby. Oh, Lacey. I love you."

Emotion flooded her. "I love you," she whispered, throat tight.

He pumped faster, his hands cradling her butt. Lacey's hips bucked, and bright lights exploded behind her eyelids. Derek's breathing grew labored as he reached his release, a sexy rumble erupting in his throat.

Long minutes later, they kissed and cuddled beneath her summer duvet. Lacey's heart raced with the joy and newness of their pairing. Her head rested on his shoulder. She snuggled her cheek against his warm chest as they whispered plans and dreams for their future.

He kissed the tip of her nose and slipped out of bed. "I'll be back soon."

"Where are you going?" Lacey murmured in a drowsy voice.

"The champagne. We're not done celebrating."

"Good idea." She balanced on an elbow, gazing at his naked rear as he left. Then she flopped onto her pillow, a wrist across her forehead. She stared at the intersection of four ceiling tiles. "Wow," she whispered. She'd blurted she was falling in love, and Derek hadn't run screaming from the room. No, he'd returned her rapidly growing feelings, and they'd spoken about a life together.

She couldn't wait for every single stage of their future to unfold.

As the sound of his footfalls neared her bedroom again, memories of last Friday night at the police station engulfed her. She had been riding high on nerves and excitement, heart pounding and hands shaking as she'd approached his desk. Then he'd glanced up, and her heart had caved in on itself.

She'd attributed her emotional response to the prospect of finagling Janie's brother to the bachelorette party and winning the scavenger hunt. Now she realized that a forceful bolt of insta-love had bopped her between the eyes. And she couldn't be happier.

In another moment, the man responsible for the biggest and most wonderful surprise of her life sauntered into the bedroom. He held the crystal flutes, a corkscrew, and the champagne bottle. Lacey blinked. And, oh my God, he wore the scarlet G-string—the one he'd tossed onto her bread box—around his neck!

She laughed. "Derek! What on earth?"

His eyebrows wiggled. "I thought I'd introduce you to my dorky side."

She gazed at his remarkable physique, her body warming as her glance lingered on his semi-hard arousal. "I like your dorky side."

The damn thing twitched.

Derek looked down at his body part. "I told you in the kitchen," he said in a commanding voice.

"This time around, Lacey and I are having champagne first." His gaze lifted. "My apologies. It's a little stubborn."

Lacey giggled. "I wouldn't say *little*." Derek wasn't kidding that he had a dorky side. He was a perfect match for her. They were perfect.

She sat up against the soft pillows and reached for the two champagne flutes.

Derek tugged on the satin thong around his neck. "I might've damaged a leg hole putting this on, but I couldn't resist doing something goofy to make you smile."

"You're forgiven," she whispered.

He stepped back and popped the champagne cork. A narrow stream of bubbles frothed over his knuckles. Lacey extended the glasses, and he filled the flutes.

"Although you ruined that pair," she declared, nodding at the thong. "Panty slayer."

"*Corporate* panty slayer," he corrected, giving her another kiss.

He put the bottle on the nightstand and dried his hands with his T-shirt from the floor. Lacey predicted a load of laundry in their future. But for now...

She threw back the duvet, and he climbed into bed. They clinked glasses.

"You can slay my panties any time," she whispered. And that was no lie.

Because while this dream of a man might have stolen her underwear, he'd also stolen her heart.

Don't miss the next book in the series, *Catching Claire*, featuring Ridge Pederson, the dancer from the bachelorette party, and Claire Merriweather, the maid of honor for the upcoming wedding! (If it happens...)

Note: Catching Claire begins a few hours following the bachelorette party in Deceiving Derek.

Get your copy of *Catching Claire*!

The story:

When Claire Merriweather hires sexy future doctor Ridge Pederson to strip at a friend's bachelorette party, she never imagines she'll wake up in his bed.

Well, she *imagines* it—but now it's happened.

Big problem: Claire's memory is fuzzy. *Did* they do the bouncy or did Ridge reject her?

Either way...uh-oh, her heart is in trouble!

Catching Claire Preview
Steamy RomCom
by Cindy Procter-King

Just after midnight, Saturday, July 15th
Countdown to Tania and Trey's wedding: 14 days
(unless...)

Stripping off his clothes in a room packed with rowdy women was not Ridge Pederson's idea of a good time. But how could he refuse when the gigs paid a nice portion of his medical school bills?

Ridge exited the elevator, patting the coins in the pocket of the PJ pants riding low on his hips. As he strode toward the apartment building's laundry, the sour scent of alcohol lifted from his clothesbasket. His nose wrinkled. Over the last month, raucous bachelorette parties had crammed his summer weekends. Women pawed him, stumbled against his naked chest, 'forgot' to tip him. Or the big winner—they puked on his lap.

Thankfully, no one had upchucked during tonight's job, although the future bride had offered him a sip from her sticky cup, sprinkling his cop costume.

Ridge shouldered into the laundry room, balancing the hamper beneath an arm. Several feet away, a curvy brunette wriggled her bounteous booty in front of the bulletin board. Ridge peered at her. Claire Merriweather? The polite beauty who'd hired him for tonight's festivities danced in a short purple nightie that did wonders for her shapely thighs. As she bopped on spiky sandals, she tucked a messy wave of chocolate-brown hair behind one ear. Two dangling cords likely attached to a phone tucked...somewhere interesting, he'd bet.

She must own one super-tiny phone.

The sight of Claire dancing without a care in the world almost made up for tonight's annoyances. Almost.

Because her singing sucked.

The heavy door slammed shut as Ridge walked past her jiggling butt. He placed his hamper on the first washing machine. Throughout his performance in a fourth-floor apartment of this same building, Claire had arranged snacks and mixed drinks in the tiny kitchen. Then, she'd worn a simple white blouse tucked into jeans. Her courteous voicemail reserving his services in no way matched this animated dancing. Purple panties peeked from the hem of her floaty top. She swung a plastic cup and belted questionable lyrics.

"I copped a feel and then kissed it! Oh, yeah. Oh, yeah," Claire sang in a peel-the-paint-off-the-walls soprano. "The tip of his—la, la—nightstick!" Her cup rocked. The creamy concoction splashed onto the floor beside a humming dryer.

"Hello," Ridge called.

Her eyelids flitted half-open. She patted an earbud and continued her mangled version of karaoke.

"Hello!" Ridge strode toward her, thumping the washers.

Her gaze riveted to the bulletin board.

He cursed. Any loser might waltz in and see her. Take advantage of her. Maybe attack her.

Claire licked a flyer pinned to the cork. *Licked* it!

He stood behind her as she tongued the ad a second time. *His* ad. For his stripping business.

In the flyer, he wore the cop costume she'd

requested for the party. Stainless-steel handcuffs dangled from his thick black belt, and he gripped a strategically positioned nightstick.

Singing, Claire Merriweather tore off every tab. She stuffed the papers into the frilly material at her cleavage.

Ridge narrowed his gaze. His second summer of med school was in full swing, and he'd worked his ass off to achieve his dream of becoming a doctor. *Nobody* messed with his tuition money.

Voice harsh, he tapped her shoulder. "Excuse me?"

Claire shrieked and jumped. Her drink flew out of the cup, splashing the flyer. One earbud popped free, and the cord swung around her bare shoulders.

"Sorry!" Ridge's hands shot up. What was he thinking, touching a customer, startling her? "I hit the washers to catch your attention—"

A loopy grin split Claire Merriweather's face. "It's you! My cop-a-feel!" She plopped the cup onto the droning dryer and flung her arms around his neck. Her lush breasts crushed his T-shirt, and a sweet whiff of Irish Cream liqueur drifted from her lips.

Ridge pushed her an arm's-length away and held her there. Not that he didn't appreciate her enthusiasm. In fact, a part of his anatomy appreciated it *too* much.

"You were at the bachelorette party tonight," he reminded her, in case her neurons had misfired. "You hired me for your friend, Tania. I danced with her in Alicia Maxwell's apartment. Remember?"

Claire lifted a shoulder. "I wouldn't say I hired you for Tania."

Ridge flicked his gaze over her cute-as-hell attire. The tabs with his phone number fluttered from inside her top. Her purple nightwear—baby dolls, that was it—featured wide shoulder straps. Slippery fabric nipped at her waist and flared at her hips. He liked the tiny white bows dotting the hem. He liked the large bow centered on her cleavage even more.

That said, up close, on a spicy scale of one to ten, Claire's loungewear rated a three. The neckline didn't plunge, and the skirt covered her ass—when she wasn't bouncing around. The papers poking out of her top and the dangling cord gave her the appearance of a sexy, disorganized burglar on a midnight heist.

"Yes," he stated. "You hired me to dance for Tania Hoyt. She's the bride." He hadn't gyrated his hips for the wrong woman throughout his performance, had he? Impossible. Someone would have complained.

"I 'member," Claire slurred, and her beguiling dimples flashed. "Hey. Do ya twit?" She giggled. "How about video posts? You'd get a ton more calls."

Ridge's grip on her upper arms slackened. His social media game was bang-on, but that wasn't the point. "If you hadn't destroyed my *ad*, I'd get all the bookings I need."

Her gaze lowered to his plaid flannels, which he wore commando.

She looked back up, her pale green irises shining. "You pack quite a package, Ridge."

He rolled his eyes. *May lightning strike me dead. Now. I'll donate my body to science.*

Two weeks ago, when Claire hired him, her voice on the phone had sounded practical. Sensible. They'd discussed his rates and his arrival time at Alicia Maxwell's apartment, the duration and heat level of his performance. He had no problem flirting with partygoers or stripping down to a leather G-string. Unlike some event dancers, he drew the line at simulating sex with the guest of honor. In tonight's case, Claire's friend, Tania.

"You're steadier on your feet now," he said, releasing Claire's shoulders.

Her hands slipped beneath his T-shirt. *Jeez!* Her palms skated over his abs and pecs. His flannels risked tenting in an energetic salute.

"Do me," she whispered.

"Stop." Clutching her wrists, Ridge flipped her hands back out. "Claire, I don't know what you think I'm advertising"—other than the party dances—"but I will not sleep with you." Or any other client.

Her lips pursed, and his dick twitched. God help him.

"Not even if I leave a generous tip?"

"What?" Was she for real? *"No."*

She pouted. "What's wrong with me?"

"Nothing. I don't pick up drunk women." Between the med-school grind and grabbing whatever work fit his busy schedule, he hadn't gotten laid in longer than he cared to consider. And she'd needed to remind him?

"I'm. Not. Drunk." Her bleary gaze indicated otherwise.

He released her wrists. "It doesn't matter."

She wobbled on her sandals. "You won't take me home?" She stomped a heel. "No one ever takes me home! No one says I'm beautiful. Everybody thinks I'm fat. No one loves me. Everyone loves Tania.

Everyone loves Lacey. Alicia's dog worships *her*. But I'm unlovable!"

"You're not unlovable. And you're not fat." Not every guy wanted to date a human pogo stick.

Claire jutted a hip. "Would we have sex if I were five-seven and had great boobs?"

Ridge trained his gaze on her face. "You do have great boobs." From what he'd noticed moments ago.

"You're not looking at them. You're not feeling them." She launched herself forward. "Catch!"

"Careful!" He pushed out his hands—and her generous rack filled his palms.

Her loopy grin returned. "There. Now tell me they aren't great."

"I never said they weren't great." Ridge's throat tightened. Claire's breasts spilled over his fingers. Firm yet soft. Perfection.

Don't look down.

He looked down.

His thumbs nudged the center bow on her top. His fingers pressed the papers against the ivory skin above her modest neckline.

Look back up, Pederson. Don't squeeze these babies. Not even once.

Claire slumped against his chest, and her temple banged his chin.

He squinted. "Claire?" But her mouth had relaxed with sleep, her eyes sealed shut.

He groaned. She'd passed out with her hot knockers stuffing his hands.

What the hell did he do now?

Picture Imperfect Preview
Steamy Mystery Romance
by Cindy Procter-King

Just when she thought she had her life on autofocus...

Ursula Scott is barreling full-steam ahead with plans to buy a photography studio. She can put up with a few things going wonky, until...

Half-naked dudes show up for her first-ever shoot for a major magazine.

Plus, it looks like someone is sabotaging the business.

Suddenly, she realizes her sexy apprentice is an ex-cop working the case undercover—and *she's* a suspect!

by Cindy Procter-King

Gabe McKenzie has his hands full with Ursula's need to clear her name and play amateur sleuth. How can he convince her to stop snooping around and let him do *his* job as a PI before an unknown menace threatens not only her dreams...but her life?

Chapter One

If Ursula Scott had to look at one more naked man, she'd scream.

Loud and long.

Case in point, the cocky fifty-year-old adjusting his thong as he trundled toward the photography studio's tiny dressing room.

Shuddering, Ursula turned away. Okay, the guy wasn't *totally* nude but close enough. Their session was a memory she could live without. As were several appointments from this morning.

She lifted the camera strap over her head and carefully set her professional Nikon on the prop table. Behind her, the dressing room door clicked shut. Ursula narrowed her gaze.

Damn her boss, Victor McKenzie, hiding in his office. It didn't take a Mensa membership to figure out what he was up to—avoiding the questionable applicants responding to the model ad *he'd* placed in a Seattle print and online newspaper.

After the recent rash of vandalism the studio had experienced, Ursula really needed something in her life to run smoothly. Was it asking too much for that thing to be the test shots for her first magazine photo spread?

She spun her silver thumb ring. Six months from now, in May, she would buy Mackie's studio. Every assignment she completed in the interim would cement her chances of building a profitable business and assisting her parents with their massive debt. Her dad wouldn't accept her help any other way. Neither would her mom. Ursula needed to secure her future first, they said. No, insisted. And she was trying! With everything in her.

But sometimes working for Victor McKenzie, once a talented photographer whose industry contacts would transfer to her with the sale, tested her last nerve.

At a scuffing sound, she glanced toward the hall door. Stacy, the part-time receptionist, scurried in carrying the pumpkin-spiced latte Ursula had requested from the coffee shop next door. No foam, extra-hot.

Stacy handed over the latte, and Ursula's finger-tips stung as she grasped the cardboard cup.

"Sorry I'm late." Stacy adjusted her black-rimmed glasses. "Eighteen more potential models are waiting to see you. I wrote their info on the appointment sheets, super-legible like you asked. It took a while."

"Thanks. I appreciate it." Ursula refused to treat the night-school student with Mackie's surly brand of disrespect. At twenty, Stacy was eager, organized, and a lifesaver on busy days.

"We're getting tons of calls about the test shots." Stacy pumped a fist. "It's only Wednesday, and we're booking into next week."

Ursula sighed. "We have to draw the line somewhere, Stace. I know *Seattle Lights* asked us to test everyone who responds to the ad, but at this rate we won't narrow the field in time." To accommodate the production window for the magazine's popular Valentine's issue, *Seattle Lights* required the "Real Men, Real Lives, Real Loves" photo spread completed by December. The rush job allowed Ursula two days to finish the preliminary shots and barely two weeks to photograph the eight men the editor would select from a shortlist.

Stacy's eyebrows bunched. "Should I talk to Mackie about it?"

"No. I will later." This morning's applicants weren't Stacy's concern. Leaning forward, Ursula whispered, "Tell me, are they all as sleazy-looking as...?" She nodded toward the changing room, where the thong monster had vanished.

Stacy shook her head, whispering back, "Some actually seem quite normal. And this one guy? I *so* want to take down his info."

"Go on."

"Tall. Six-two or -three," Stacy murmured. "Shoulders like a linebacker. Slim hips, trim waist. I'm thinking awesome abs." She crossed her fingers. "Masses of wavy dark hair. On his head. It's almost black, like yours, but with a rich chestnut brown mixed in. Great butt too. Hot, hot."

"Sounds promising." Ursula sipped her latte, and warmth curled in her tummy. "A variation in attitude is what I'm after. All this strutting around is growing tiresome." She wrinkled her nose.

Stacy giggled. "At least Mackie's letting you run the shoot, Urs. That's major."

Last week, when their boss had dangled the carrot, Ursula would have agreed. After what had felt like eons of toiling at small jobs to improve the studio's bottom line while he lazed around during the year of their agreement, finally the chance had arrived to showcase her skills to a significant client.

However, as she'd learned, Mackie's good deeds usually carried a downside. And *this* one was a doozy. A day after passing her the assignment, he'd let it slip that he'd skipped over obtaining her input on publicizing the call for models featuring the new Real Men angle, which he'd also failed to mention before, and now any dude and his doohickey could saunter in for the test shots.

So much for the *GQ* types Mackie had vowed would pose in front of her camera. Yeah, he was her employer, but how could he *not* pass on the correct information?

She wiped a palm on her jeans. The dressing room door opened, and the thong fellow emerged, wearing a sweater and baggy slacks.

The man shrugged into a jacket. "When will I learn if you're using me?"

"Calls will go out Monday, Mr. Hacklemire. Thanks for coming in." Ursula pasted on a smile until he left. Placing her latte on the table, she told Stacy, "Please send in the next guy. The sooner I complete this round, the sooner I can forget this day ever happened."

"Want the hottie first?" the girl asked, heading out.

"No, it's best to stick with the order of arrival. I wouldn't want to aggravate the mob." Ursula looped the Nikon around her neck. A minute later, as she adjusted lights and flash reflectors, the studio door opened and closed.

"Where do you want me, honey?" A sturdy man sporting a burgundy satin dressing robe stood inside the vast room. Sneakers shod his sock-less feet, and enough coarse black hair to outfit ten shaved monkeys forested his bare shins and partially exposed upper chest. "Name any position you like. I'm very limber." One of his eyebrows drooped in an obscene wink, and he curled his lips in what Ursula assumed he considered a sexy look.

Uh, *nope.*

"It's not just lounge-wear shots," she responded in a cool voice. This guy had shown up at her *place of business* not wearing pants? Unless he'd changed in the studio restroom near her boss's office, he must have.

She was two seconds from losing it!

The man stepped closer, hoisting a gym bag. "I brought my other gear along. Thought we'd start with my best look first."

Repressing the urge to roll her eyes, she accepted his information slip and scanned it. "Make yourself comfortable, Mr. Longfellow." She stacked the paper beneath the cat-shaped paperweight on the table. "I'll take your bag until you need to change for the shirts-on shots." She reached for his pack. *Big* mistake. He dropped the duffel and planted his hands on his hips.

His robe parted to reveal gold satin boxers with a gaping fly.

A gaping, *inhabited* fly.

She gulped, and some movement occurred.

Too much movement occurred.

The creep's creep was creeping out!

He winked again. "Mr. *Long*fellow."

"*What are you doing*?" Ursula flung up her hands, shielding her gaze for a merciful split-second.

"Just making an impact on ya', babe. There's a lot of competition out there."

"I don't care if the Sexiest Man Alive is out there! I'm not taking your picture today. Or ever!"

"I don't get my chance like everyone else?"

"You blew your chance when you perved yourself, buster. Get out of my studio!"

He lifted his hands, and the bathrobe fell closed. "Don't throw a chick-fit. I'm going."

"You bet your shortfellow you are." Ursula policed the dude to the reception area, her camera bumping her abdomen with every stride. Stacy's head popped up from the desk. Ursula escorted the creeper through the noisy throng and out onto the street. Chilly air swept in as she locked the glass door behind him. No way, no *how*, were more scum-bags getting in.

She whirled to face the inappropriately dressed men milling around Stacy's desk. The scent of sweaty armpits permeated the air.

"Listen up!" Several heads snapped toward her. She pointed to the door. "If anyone else thinks this is a porno gig, they can leave. 'No-shirts shots' does not mean 'no-sense-of-common-decency shots.' If I see another piece of spandex or satin enter my studio, I'll hit the roof." She was up there already!

"I brought swim trunks. They're nylon," a Vin Diesel look-alike shouted. "That work?"

"Bermudas here!"

"Jeans."

"Sweats."

"Are mankinis made of spandex?"

Ursula clutched her thumping forehead. "I'm taking ten. Everyone clear your wardrobes through Stacy."

She stalked toward the main hall to the right of Reception. The male crowd parted as if she were an ovary-laden Moses commanding the Red Sea. She glimpsed linebacker shoulders and chestnut hair as she stormed past, but she wasn't in the mood for sightseeing. Right now, she didn't give a crap about anything but ripping off Mackie's head.

The heels of her shoes thundered on the worn linoleum. "Mackie!" She shoved his door. *Stuck.* She shoulder-rammed it. The old doorknob sprang loose, and she pushed inside the cluttered horror of Victor McKenzie's office.

Tinny music blared from a prehistoric transistor radio topping the bookshelf beneath the blind-drawn window. Mackie sat behind his gigantic desk, chomping a submarine sandwich.

Apparently, he wasn't the only one enjoying a snack. Red spiked pumps poked out from beneath the desk bottom. A female voice cooed, praising his proportions.

Ursula's stomach roiled. *Oh, God, not Jasmine?* His latest girlfriend.

She stepped back. "Sorry!" Really, really, *really* sorry.

The sandwich dropped to the desk. "Ursula? What the hell?" Mackie jumped up, hands scrambling for his zipper—and Ursula uttered a prayer of thanks that he wasn't a tall man.

A bonking sound echoed beneath the desk. "Ow, my head."

Ursula raced into the hall, camera bouncing. "Mackie, lock your door!" She slammed it shut.

"It was!" His gruff voice blasted through the partition.

"Then fix it. With a deadbolt."

"Don't be so judgmental! You never heard of Hump Day?"

Gabe McKenzie clenched his jaw against the dull ache from his injury gripping his ass. After seven years with the LAPD, rowdy crowds shouldn't rile him, but the scene in his low-life uncle's photography studio rivaled anything he'd experienced in California.

"Do you mind giving a guy some room?" Nudging a fellow in frayed jean shorts, Gabe signaled the girl at the reception desk. He'd returned to Seattle three days ago and had a physical therapy appointment this afternoon he couldn't miss. If his mom hadn't begged him to check out vandalism and threats at her brother-in-law's studio, Gabe wouldn't have ventured *near* Victor McKenzie Photography.

He signaled the girl again. Her attention

remained riveted to the men clustered around her desk.

Gabe shook his head. Forget a polite request. He'd follow the raven-haired photographer who'd shouted his uncle's name as she'd charged down the main corridor moments ago, camera bobbing.

Moving slowly so he wouldn't strain his stiff right glute, Gabe passed around the corner and into a hall decorated with framed portraits. The photographer strode toward him now, her dark eyebrows furrowed. Behind her, an office door rattled on squeaking hinges.

Spotting him, she stopped dead in her tracks. "You shouldn't be back here."

"I need to see Vic."

She winced. "He's with someone."

"Then I'll wait. Here. But I won't return to that zoo." Gabe jabbed a thumb toward the waiting room.

"You don't have a choice, Mr.—"

"Gabe."

Her frown eased. In fact, for an instant, her full mouth tipped into an expression someone desperate for affection might mistake for a smile.

"I'm sorry, Gabe. Seeing Mr. McKenzie won't

bump you to the head of the line. I'm in charge of the Real Men shoot, not him."

"I'm not here to have my picture taken." With a practiced eye honed by years on the job, Gabe catalogued her appearance in three heartbeats: around twenty-five, straight black hair hanging past her shoulders, white blouse tucked into jeans, chunky belt. Thick lashes framed dark blue eyes he wouldn't mind waking up to. Her left thumb sported a thick ring of hammered silver, the right pinky a slim gold band. What his salon-obsessed desk sergeant in Los Angeles would call a French manicure highlighted long fingernails that could easily emasculate a guy were he dumb enough to land on her bad side.

And this photographer no doubt *had* a bad side.

Man, even ticked off, she was stunning.

"Vic McKenzie is my uncle," he said.

Her gaze zipped over him. "You're kidding."

Gabe didn't require psychic abilities to read her mind—no family resemblance whatsoever. Vic stood maybe five-six, with a belly as round as a giant panda's. His hook nose, brown eyes, and olive skin bore traces of his Sicilian heritage.

"My dad was his brother," Gabe explained. "My grandparents adopted Vic as a toddler."

"Oh." Ursula looked confused.

"Vic isn't so bad. In small doses." Once a decade would suit this nephew. "I can't imagine it's a thrill working for him though."

She snorted. "Now you understand my problem." She lifted a hand. "Sorry. Gabe, I don't want to insult your uncle, but I'm having a horrible day. Someone screwed up the model ad for the magazine shoot, and I'm pretty sure it was Mackie. We wanted everyday Joes, so the state of their bodies isn't the issue. It's the state of their undress." She cringed.

"Undress?"

"The shorts. The tightie-whities. The thongs. The ad was supposed to read 'shirts off,' not 'leave your inhibitions at home.' Your uncle is lucky I'm not quitting here and now." She twirled her gold pinky ring. "But I *can't* quit, which he well knows."

"Look. I understand your frustration with my uncle, Ms.—"

"Scott. Ursula Scott."

"I really do need to see him. I promised my mom."

Her gaze lingered on the old T-shirt he wore beneath a battered leather jacket. She rested a hand on her large camera lens. "If you're Mackie's nephew, why haven't we met before?" she asked, looking him in the eyes. "I've worked here since May."

That deep, mesmerizing blue reached inside him. "Just moved back to town. Vic and I aren't close, but he's tight with my mom." Who kindly ignored the seedy aspects of her brother-in-law's life. The strip joints and endless women. Vic had placed Gabe's mom on a pedestal for as long as Gabe remembered. Vic remained on his best behavior around her, and she treated him like a younger brother. Her last link to Gabe's dad.

"Can you help me out?" he asked the photographer.

She chewed the inside of her cheek, mouth twisting. "The thing is, I'm not sure when he'll be free. Like I said, he's in a meeting."

The office door opened. A late-thirties blond woman in a neon-pink mini-skirt, orange jean jacket, spiked red heels, and layers of makeup pranced out. Ursula glanced over her shoulder as the new arrival sashayed toward them.

The woman dug into her purse. "He's all yours," she said to Ursula, juggling a lipstick and retrieving a small mirror. She opened the mirror, pushed out her bottom lip like a fish going for a lure, and smeared on bright pink lip color. She beamed at Gabe. "Hi. I'm Jasmine, Mackie's girlfriend."

"Hi. Gabe. Nephew."

"Cool."

"Sorry for barging in on you," Ursula muttered to Jasmine, avoiding the woman's gaze.

"That's okay. I was taking an early lunch." Jasmine returned her stuff to her purse. "Oh." Her long fingers danced on Ursula's upper arm. "Before I forget, Mackie says Brinley's Hardware sells the best deadbolts. He wants you to get that Stacy girl to buy him a new one."

Ursula's gaze flashed. "He can tell her himself. Unbelievable."

"He's a little busy right now."

"Oh, yeah?" Red flared high on Ursula's cheeks. "Well, I'm a whole lot *disgusted* right now. With him. You know, Jasmine, if you like being Mackie's carrier pigeon so much, feel free to tell him that I'm returning to the studio to finish today's test shots. It's not the fault of the men waiting in Reception if the ad got royally messed up. *Then* I'm heading home. For the rest of the day. And maybe the rest of the year." Her voice rose. "If Mackie wants me to finish this shoot, he needs to come up with some fantastic incentive. I want my name listed on the photo credits, not his. I want complete creative control."

Jasmine blinked. "How can I tell him all that? I don't understand half of what you said."

"Forget it. I don't expect you to remember anything." Ursula's eyes closed. "Jasmine, I apologize. It's my issue, not yours. I'll tell him."

"I'll mention the deadbolt," Gabe assured the woman.

"Great. I gotta go." Jasmine spun on her skyscraper heels and strutted toward a rear exit.

Clutching her camera, Ursula marched toward the waiting room at the front of the building.

"You're welcome," Gabe called after her.

She continued walking. "For what?"

"For thanking me for offering to speak to my uncle about the deadbolt."

She stopped. "I don't remember *asking* you to do anything." She strode on.

Gabe grinned. The way her ass wiggled... Had she guessed he liked its sexy curves and size? The perfect amount for his hands to—

Probably best if he kept that information to himself.

Knocking on the office door a second time, Gabe called, "Uncle Vic?"

No reply.

Opening the door, he peeked inside. Vic was asleep in his office chair. Stubby legs propped on the desktop, hairy arms dangling, head thrown back. His mouth gaped as he snored. His shoe nudged a half-eaten submarine sandwich, his lime-green sport shirt boasted hula dancers, and a scrawny ponytail scraped back his thinning salt-and-pepper hair.

Gabe shook his head. What did his mother see in the boor? After all these years, how could she still consider Vic her misguided, but harmless, brother-in-law?

Sore glute protesting, Gabe entered and closed the door. He stepped to the radio and flicked it off. "Uncle Vic?"

"Hunh?" Squinty eyes snapped open. "Whoozat? Doug?"

Gabe's father, dead over a decade.

Every time Gabe returned to Seattle, his mom said how much he and his dad looked alike at the same ages. Gabe spotted the similarities in old snap-shots and memories. From the time Gabe was three, when Dad came home for lunch, he would let Gabe wear his police hat or sit in his cruiser. During Gabe's teen years, his buddies admired the tough-but-fair cop.

Gabe would never stop missing his dad. He'd grown up wanting to emulate him. Had followed in his footsteps when choosing a career. More than anything, he'd wanted to make his dad proud.

"It's Gabe, your nephew." He limped to the guest chair and sat.

Vic stretched, and his stocky legs slid off the desk. "Right." Then, as if realizing he hadn't sounded overjoyed, he added, "Good to see ya'. When'd you get in?"

"Sunday. My stuff is in storage until I find a place. I'm staying with Mom in the meantime."

Vic bit into the sub. "Finally had enough of LA, huh?" he asked around a full mouth.

"I think LA has had enough of me."

Vic guffawed, and a soggy bread chunk flew onto the floor. "Yeah, Evie said you caught a bullet in the keister." His expression sobered. "She was plenty broke up about it. Reminded her of Doug."

"I know." Gabe's chest tightened. "She doesn't need more heartache in her life, Uncle Vic. So I'm home for good."

His uncle sucked on the straw of a take-out cup. "How old are you now?"

"Thirty in a few months."

"Kind of young to be out of commission. Although I guess they gave you a huge chunk of change, huh?"

Gabe ignored the question about his medical pension. "I might not feel fast enough to work the streets, but that doesn't mean I'm leaving the life completely. I'm opening a private investigations firm."

"No more brown-nosing the brass. Sounds good," Vic said in his troll-munching-gravel voice. "I never understood how your dad tolerated that shit."

Gabe's shoulders stiffened. "First off, I don't suck up to my bosses. Second, I'd rather not talk about Dad." His father had died a decorated narcotics detective after twenty years with the Seattle City Police Department. His memory deserved Vic's respect.

Vic chucked the remainder of his sandwich in the trashcan. "Whatever." He dusted his hands above his desk. Bread crumbs littered the office files spread over the surface.

"Listen, Uncle Vic—"

"C'mon, kid, don't call me that. 'Uncle Vic'

makes me feel like you're ten years old. Call me Mackie, like everyone else."

Gabe stretched his sore leg. "Okay...Mackie. Last night Mom said you've been having some trouble. She mentioned an inert grenade breaking the studio window a month ago?"

His uncle's beady eyes darted away. "Yeahhh."

"Did you report the incident to the police?"

"Of course. How was I to know the grenade was fake? Damn thing could've blown me up."

"The bomb squad came down?"

Vic waved a hand. "Show-offs. They couldn't tell if the grenade was fake by standing around and gawking at it, so they brought in the bomb dog and a bunch of experts. Caused a big brouhaha."

Gabe nodded. Many army surplus stores sold de-milled grenades as novelty items. While most of the units featured mangled or drilled bottoms, it was easy enough to reshape and camouflage the affected area with modeling clay and paint. Someone who knew what they were doing might even weld the holes and reactivate the units with explosive fillers and homemade fuses. No halfway competent bomb tech would rely on sight recognition to determine whether the grenade that had busted his uncle's studio window posed a threat.

"What did they find?" he asked.

His uncle—*Mackie*—frowned. "Why do you care?"

"Mom's worried."

"That Evie. So sweet." Mackie crossed his arms. "Some jerk-off stuck masking tape over the hole and painted it to make it look real enough. No finger-prints, no witnesses. Not even a security camera. The one next door went on the fritz, and the coffee shop farts wasted time 'researching options'"—he air-quoted—"before deciding to spring for an updated model. Won't get installed for three weeks. I relied on that camera. Pissed me off."

"You don't have your own security equipment?" Why was Gabe not surprised? His uncle was a tightwad from way back.

"I got lights in the alley," Mackie said. "No camera. No witnesses. Cops bellyached about both. Damn fools are useless. In the end, they said the fake grenade was probably kids getting their jollies. What do they know?"

Gabe ignored his uncle's cop rant. He was here because of his mom. "I saw a banger-type T-shirt shop next door." To the left of the studio. A coffee shop occupied the space to the right. "Do teens hang around there?"

"Yeah. Usually they ain't buying no T-shirts. They use the place as a pissing ground, the snot-nosed punks."

"What about on Halloween? Mom said you found hostile words and images painted on the waiting room display window the next morning. Something about your short and worthless life, she recalls."

Mackie rolled back his chair. "I shouldn't have worried Evie. I'll call and say I'm sorry I bothered her."

"It's too late, Uncle Vic. You told her. She knows."

"Yeah, but—"

Gabe peered at his uncle. "Tell me you reported the painted window."

"Like I'd give the cops the satisfaction! Dopes couldn't find their asses with both hands and a headlight. They found out squat about the grenade. Why would I ask them to look into some stupid graffiti that didn't hurt anyone?"

"Did you take pictures at least?" Without a witness or evidence, there was nothing the Seattle police could do.

Gabe's uncle stood. "*No.* I can see where you're going with this, kid, and it's not happening. No pictures and no calling the cops about those dumb paintings. Not then or now. I cleaned the window so my clients wouldn't see that crap. That's the last I want to hear about it."

Gabe shrugged. "It's your funeral."

Mackie grinned. "Not yet." He paused. "Your mother's really worried about me?"

"That's why I'm here."

"I guess I should have kept my mouth shut." He rubbed his palms together. "Well. Now you're home. That'll make her happy. I'm sure my troubles are over. You know, we should celebrate with a family dinner. I'll phone Evie—"

"Hold on. I met your photographer, Ursula." Gabe described the chaos in the front office. "She thinks there was some sort of problem with a model ad, and it's bringing in the wrong people."

"St. Peter on a pecker! Just when a guy thinks he can take it easy." Mackie stomped to the bookshelf and whisked a folded newspaper off a messy pile. "The ad's in the *Clarion*. Entertainment section. A big boxed ad. I shelled out for their website too, but a real paper shows class."

"Which client wants the pictures of the guys?" Gabe asked as his uncle cleared desk clutter and flattened the newspaper.

"*Seattle Lights* magazine. There's so much internet competition these days that the mag is trying a new direction with their annual pictorial. They didn't want to out themselves in the ad, so I placed it under the studio's name."

"Did you phone in the ad or fill out a website form?"

Mackie flipped pages. "Where is it?" He looked up. "Uh, no. I was gonna do it, but I had Stacy call them instead. She's the other girl. Part time." He turned more pages. "I don't believe this. It's not here. Crap almighty! I knew I should've done it myself."

"I'll look." Gabe stepped in front of his uncle and riffled through a local newspaper distributed three times a week.

Mackie paced the office, grabbing the take-out cup and slurping the contents before tossing the container into the garbage. The aromas of spicy deli meat and mustard drifted from the trashcan. "Find anything?" he asked.

"Not yet. Maybe Stacy put it in Classifieds." Gabe continued searching. "Why not advertise in the daily paper? You'd have greater circulation and exposure."

"Haven't you heard? Inflation, kid. I'm cutting back."

"Uh-huh." *Cheapskate.* "Plenty of online places are free."

"Class, kid, class. The magazine wanted a print paper. They didn't specify which."

A moment later, Gabe looked up. "Found it. In the Personals."

"What the f—?"

Gabe lifted the page. "See? A simple ad. No box, no bold print. Do you remember the wording?"

"Why?"

"Because this ad says..." Gabe read aloud, "*Looking for Real Men. Do you have what it takes to satisfy me? I want you in my spread.*" He shook his head. Who would write this junk? "*Big, short, small. Long, skinny, tall. Photographs mandatory, clothing optional. Surprise me. Call Stacy at 555-0182. Victor McKenzie Photography. We'll make you famous.*"

Mackie's bushy eyebrows pitched downward. He yanked open a drawer and flung a sheet of paper at Gabe. "Here's the *real* ad."

Gabe set down the newspaper and skimmed the ad copy, which called for everyday dudes to participate in a Valentine's Day pictorial. "*Models,*" he read, "*must feel comfortable posing without shirts for this tasteful series of photographs.*"

"Comfortable, not freaking porn freaks!"

"Someone seriously screwed up." Gabe ran a thumb along his jaw. "Maybe on purpose."

"Not *someone*, you deadbeat. Stacy. She called in the ad." Mackie pawed a hand over his sparse hair. "Now I have to arrange a retraction. Damn it to hell." He snatched the office phone receiver. "I'm gonna ream her out something good."

Gabe punched the disconnect button. "Not so fast."

Find out more at:
www.cindyprocter-king.com

Acknowledgments

Wow, I had no idea when I first wrote *Deceiving Derek* that the story would develop into a series! Or that it would take me so long to actually write that series.

But here we are. You know, shite happens.

I would like to thank my friend, Mary J. Forbes, for reading the original version of *Deceiving Derek* and for answering all my questions about the cop life. Any mistakes and embellishments are mine.

Thank you also to my readers for sticking by me through a 3-year and then a greater-than-5-year publishing break. I didn't take those breaks on purpose. Life just smacked me, and the last smack did a number on my noggin.

But, slowly, sooo slowly, I will continue to write and publish, just another turtle with a wild imagination who refuses to give up.

Turtle on!

Cindy

About the Author

Cindy Procter-King writes steamy romcoms and contemporary romances bursting with laughter and emotion. Sassy feel-good fiction!

Cindy's books are available from eBook retailers all over the world, as well as in trade paperback, some library hardcover and large print, and some foreign editions.

Cindy lives in Canada with her family, Ghost'Da Allie McBeagle, and too many grand-dogs to count.

For more on Cindy's books, visit:
www.cindyprocter-king.com

facebook.com/cindyprocterkingauthor

instagram.com/cindyprocterking

bookbub.com/authors/cindy-procter-king

x.com/cindypk

Crave another sassy romance?

www.readsassyromance.com